Timothy Shay Arthur

Uncle Ben's New-Years Gift And Other Stories

Timothy Shay Arthur

Uncle Ben's New-Years Gift And Other Stories

ISBN/EAN: 9783743373242

Manufactured in Europe, USA, Canada, Australia, Japa

Cover: Foto ©Andreas Hilbeck / pixelio.de

Manufactured and distributed by brebook publishing software (www.brebook.com)

Timothy Shay Arthur

Uncle Ben's New-Years Gift And Other Stories

UNCLE BEN'S

NEW-YEAR'S GIFT,

AND

OTHER STORIES.

By T. S. ARTHUR.

WITH ILLUSTRATIONS FROM ORIGINAL DESIGNS BY CROOME

PHILADELPHIA:
J. B. LIPPINCOTT & CO.
1864.

CONTENTS.

UNCLE BEN'S

NEW-YEAR'S GIFT.

"I THINK," said old Benjamin Hicks, a comfortable farmer, residing some fifty miles from Cincinnati, "that I'll take a little trip over to Salem, and see how Peter is coming on."

"I wish you would," replied the farmer's wife, a fine, hearty-looking old woman, with a pleasant, intelligent countenance. "I wish you would, Benjamin. There's not much to do now at home; and you can go away for a week as well as not. It will be a good opportunity to see the family, and judge of things a little from your own observation. Hannah makes a dreadful poor mouth whenever she writes."

A 2   7

"I know she does, and that's the reason why I thought of going over. There's something wrong, depend on't. Something wrong. Than Peter, there isn't a harder working or more industrious man anywhere. I'll give him credit for that. He ought to get along comfortably and lay up money. No one in the State has a finer piece of farm-land; nor one that, properly treated, ought to turn out more to the acre."

"And I can speak for Hannah," said the old lady. "I raised her, and I know that she hasn't a lazy bone in her body."

"It isn't want of industry on either side," remarked Benjamin Hicks. "The defect lies somewhere in a want of management; or in the profitable disposition of what they make. Hand-work is all very well; but it is often like rowing with one oar; there must be head-work to make the boat shoot lightly forward. Yes—yes, I must see them."

It was toward the latter part of December, a few days before Christmas, that the brief conversation, here given, took place between Benjamin Hicks and his wife. On Christmas-day, the old gentleman, true to his purpose, arrived by the stage in Salem. Soon afterward he entered the farm-house of Peter Miller, which, neither within nor without, presented an air of thrift or comfort.

A hearty welcome did Uncle Ben receive from Peter and Hannah; and also from their children. Of the latter, there were four living—three had died. The oldest of these was Ellen, a girl in her sixteenth year. Henry, just fourteen, came next. Between him and Hannah, a bright, restless, noisy creature, seven years old, there had been a brother and sister; but two small hillocks in the graveyard near by, marked the spot where their dust was mingling with its kindred dust. A baby, nearly two years old, completed the household treasures of Peter and Hannah Miller.

For a few hours after the old gentleman's arrival, the pleasure felt at his coming beamed from every countenance. Peter was talkative and cheerful, and Hannah's face was lit up with a constant succession of smiles. After supper, however, when all the children but Ellen were in bed—she sat up to help her mother with the sewing of the family—and the quiet of evening made the thoughts sober, Peter grew silent, and Hannah, as she sat at her work, now and then, sighed involuntarily.

"How are you getting on, Peter?" asked Mr. Hicks, breaking in upon a silence of several minutes.

"Not so well as I could wish, Uncle Ben," replied Peter. He tried to affect a cheerful air, but the real despondency that was in his heart could not be disguised.

"I'm sorry to hear you say that," returned the old gentleman. "You were always honest and industrious; and in this country, honest industry should rise by its own inherent buoyancy."

"Peter works hard enough, dear knows!" spoke up Hannah. "We ought to get along. If he goes on as he has been going for the last few years, he will break himself down."

"That's bad," said Uncle Ben, "very bad. Work, even hard work, is better for the health than idleness. Rust destroys more than friction. But overwork is not good."

"That I already begin to feel," said Peter. "I give out much quicker than I did some years ago."

"Bad, bad!" returned Uncle Ben, shaking his head. "You're just in the prime of life, Peter. At your age, I could go through more work, without fatigue, than at any time before."

"And what is worst of all," sighed Peter, "I don't seem to get in the least beforehand. In fact, for the last two or three years, I have found it impossible to make both ends meet."

"Yes, that is worst of all, Peter. I'm sorry to hear you speak so."

"Last winter," resumed Peter, "I lost

twenty sheep and two of the finest cows in the neighbourhood."

"We've been very unlucky, Uncle Ben," said Hannah, pausing in her work, and looking, with moistened eyes, into the old gentleman's face. "Very unlucky; and we're downright discouraged. I don't know what is going to come of us. Peter had to mortgage the farm this year."

"Mortgage! mortgage!" The old man shook his head and looked serious.

"There was no help for it, uncle," said Peter. "It was mortgage or be sued."

"How came you to get in debt?"

"Well, I bought from a neighbour a wagon and a pair of horses for a hundred and sixty dollars, promising to pay for them after harvest. But crops were short, and my bills at the store a great deal higher than I expected. In fact, there had been no settlement for a year, and it took my five hundred bushels of wheat and three hundred bushels of corn to make all square."

"Bless me!" ejaculated the old man.

"And so nothing remained to live on until next harvest?"

"Nothing."

Uncle Ben shook his head, compressed his lips, and was silent for some moments.

"What did you get for your wheat?" he at length asked.

"Fifty-eight cents," replied Peter.

"Sixty-eight."

"No; fifty-eight."

"You didn't sell your crop for that, surely?"

"Yes. It was all Gray & Elder would allow me for it."

"Fifty-eight cents! Well, that beats all! And did you sell your whole five hundred bushels at that price?"

"Yes."

"While I received sixty-eight cents for all of mine!"

"You did?"

"Certainly I did. So you lost just fifty dollars on your wheat-crop by not getting the market-price!"

"Fifty dollars! How many comforts fifty dollars would buy!" said Hannah, letting her work fall in her lap with a gesture of despondency.

"And what price did you get for your corn?" asked Uncle Ben.

"Twenty-five cents," replied Peter.

"From Gray & Elder?"

"Yes."

"Mine brought thirty-two. Just seven cents a bushel difference. How many bushels had you?"

"I sold three hundred bushels."

"At a loss of twenty-one dollars. Seventy-one dollars loss on your wheat and corn crops in a single year. I don't much wonder, Peter, that you can't get along, if you let other people swindle you in this way. It requires two things to make a successful farmer. Intelligence in agricultural matters, sufficient to make the ground produce freely, and that knowledge in regard to the state of the produce-market necessary to insure sales at the best prices.

You are a hard-working man, Peter; but, to insure success, something beyond hard work is needed. The head must guide the hands. And in order to do this, the head must be properly enlightened."

Uncle Ben inquired still further and more minutely into Peter's affairs, and the result confirmed his first impression. There was industry, but it was not enlightened industry.

"Do you take an agricultural paper?" he asked, during the conversation.

"No," replied Peter, with some emphasis. "I don't believe in book-farming. I've seen too many men ruin themselves by new experiments. I was brought up by one of the best practical farmers in the State, and know my business thoroughly. There's only one right way to till the ground, and I flatter myself that I understand that way."

Uncle Benjamin Hicks tried to show Peter that he was in error here; but this was a subject on which Peter grew warm at once, and thus closed the avenues of his mind to all the appeals of reason.

On the next day, Peter Miller was absent on business which called him to a neigh-bouring town, and the old gentleman spent most of the time in the house with his niece, asking questions, giving advice, and minutely observing every thing that passed around him. There was but little real com-fort in the dwelling, and little cultivation in the children.

Ellen, the oldest, was a coarse, hard-working girl, who had been to school long enough to learn to read and to fill a few pages of blank paper with pot-hooks and hangers. Beyond this, her mind was un-educated in all that pertained to book know-ledge. Coarse and rough as she was, how-ever, there were about her certain elements of womanly beauty in the first efforts of development, that Uncle Ben perceived, and which awoke for her, in his mind, a feeling of both interest and concern.

"You're working Ellen too hard," said

the old gentleman to his niece, as the girl passed through the room where they were sitting, carrying a large kettle of boiling water, which she had just heated for washing.

"I know it," replied Mrs. Miller; "I think of it every day. Ellen ought to be going to school. But I can't spare her. If we could afford help, it would be different. It makes my heart ache, Uncle Ben, whenever I think of the way our children are growing up."

"All bad—very bad," said Uncle Ben, shaking his head, and looking grave. "There's something wrong. Depend upon it, Ellen, there's something wrong. You're all industrious enough; all, in fact, overworked; and yet there is no thrift; no order in your family; no cheerfulness; no comfort."

Hannah acknowledged, with tears in her eyes, the truth of the picture. But she knew no remedy; and saw nothing but trouble ahead.

"If we go on as we have been going,"
said she, "we'll lose our farm in two or
three years; and then what is to become
of us all? I feel utterly discouraged."

"I see no books about," said Uncle Ben,
some time afterward. "Don't Ellen and
Henry spend some of their time in reading?"

"There's the Bible and some old reli-
gious books up-stairs," replied Hannah.
"But the children don't care about them.
Henry borrowed the Arabian Nights and
Robinson Crusoe from some of our neigh-
bours' children, and he and Ellen got so interested in them that they couldn't do any
thing else. Henry would leave his work in
the field and hide away among the bushes to
read, and Ellen would neglect every thing
for the same purpose. Their father got so angry about it, that he positively forbade their
bringing any more books into the house."

"Is it possible! You take a newspaper?"

"No. We can't afford to spend money

in that way. We have nothing to spare for useless things. And, besides, Peter has no time to read. When night comes, he is so worn down with work that he is glad to get in bed."

" No newspaper? Why, Hannah! You had much better all go without a meal once a week, than not have a newspaper. I don't wonder"——

Uncle Ben checked himself, and became more thoughtful than before.

On the next day he asked Peter why he didn't take a paper.

" No time to read; and, besides, I can't afford the expense," replied Peter.

" A couple of dollars a year would meet that."

" I must pay my debts, Uncle Ben, before I think about indulging in newspapers," returned Peter.

"You'd find a paper a great saving, even if it cost ten dollars a year," remarked the old gentleman.

Peter did not in the least comprehend the

meaning of this declaration. But as he did not ask for any explanation, none was given.

"You're a hard-working man, Peter," said Benjamin Hicks, after two or three days had been spent in the family of his nephew and niece—"a hard-working man. I'll give you credit for that. But from all I have seen and heard since I've been here, Peter, I must say that you are not a good farmer!"

"You're the first man who ever said that!" quickly replied Peter, the blood springing to his face.

"That may be," returned Uncle Ben. "Still, it does not gainsay my words. You are not a good farmer, Peter, and your want of thrift shows it."

"I wish you would explain yourself, Uncle Ben," said Peter, both his voice and countenance showing that the remark hurt him a good deal. "No man in the neighbourhood would like to say as much."

"A good farmer, with one hundred acres

of land like yours, must get along. You
don't get along; and therefore I say, you
are not a good farmer."

Now Peter was rather quick-tempered,
and this assertion of the old man chafed
him in a tender place. He tried to control
his feelings, but the effort was not fully
successful.

"Uncle Ben," said he, in a sharp, angry
voice, while his face grew still redder, "I
won't let anybody talk to me after this
fashion. I'm sorry you came, if it was only
to insult me in my troubles."

"O Peter!" exclaimed Hannah, in tones
of distress, "don't speak so to Uncle
Ben!"

"Peter—Peter," said Uncle Benjamin,
soothingly; "you don't understand me."

"Yes, I do understand you!" replied the
excited Peter. "I've got ears and common sense. You say I'm no farmer, and
that's"——

"Stop, stop, Peter. I didn't say you
were no farmer. I only said you were not

a good farmer. And if you will hear me patiently, I'll prove to you"——

"I'll hear nothing more on the subject, Uncle Ben," sharply retorted Peter. "Not a word more! When a man says I'm no farmer, I feel insulted. He might as well say that I'm not a man!"

"Peter, Peter! don't act so!" said poor Hannah, whose eyes were filling with tears. From the hour of Uncle Ben's arrival, she had suffered the hope which then sprang up in her heart, that he would help them in their troubles, to grow stronger and stronger. The many inquiries he made, and the interest he manifested in every member of the family, satisfied her that a purpose to aid them was in his mind. Now her husband seemed in a fair way to mar all by his untimely anger.

"Come, come, Peter!" spoke up the old gentleman, with some authority in his manner, "this is all nonsense. What I say is for your good. Can't you under-stand that, you silly fellow?"

"I don't wish to talk any more on the subject, Uncle Ben," replied Peter; "so change it, if you please."

This was said in a way that Uncle Ben did not by any means like; so, tossing his head with affected indifference, he answered—

"Oh, very well! very well! Just as you like."

Then came a long silence, which was finally broken by sobs from Hannah, who, after having tried for some time, but in vain, to control her feelings, burst into a fit of crying.

Neither husband nor uncle said any thing to soothe her distress.

In a little while she arose and left the room; and, in a few minutes afterward, the two men separated.

On the next morning, Uncle Ben announced, while they were at the breakfast-table, his purpose to leave for home after dinner. Peter felt sorry for having exhibited so much angry impatience, though he

partly justified himself on the plea of great
provocation. The declaration that he was
not a good farmer was one that he could
not bear. If there was any thing that he
did know, it was how to farm. On this
knowledge he had prided himself for years;
and what was more, particularly prided
himself on being a thorough practical agri-
culturist, and no "upstart theoretical book-
farmer," who, as he sometimes said, didn't
know, except for books and newspapers,
whether potatoes grew above or below
ground.

Still Peter felt sorry for having lost his
temper, and wished that it hadn't been
so. But men of his character are not apt
to own a fault. It takes a man of some
stamina, besides a good degree of self-
knowledge and true elevation of character,
to do this. He felt sorry, but not prepared
to say so.

"I thought you were going to spend a
week with us?" said Peter, when this an-
nouncement was made.

"I did think of doing so when I left home," replied the old gentleman; "but I've changed my m..nd."

Hannah looked sadly into Uncle Ben's face, and then glanced toward her husband. She did not venture to speak—her heart was too full.

Nothing more was said during the meal. After breakfast, Peter went out to look after the cattle, sheep, and horses, and Uncle Ben went into the little spare room, where a bright fire had been kindled by Ellen. He had been sitting here only a few minutes, when Hannah came in, and, drawing a chair close up to the old gentleman, said, in a choking voice, as she took his hand and looked into his face—

"Don't be angry with Peter, uncle."

"Bless you, child!" replied the old man, quickly, betraying considerable emotion as he spoke; "I am not angry with Peter."

"Oh yes, you are, and I don't much wonder. He didn't speak right. But you know how he prides himself on being a good farmer."

"I know—I know. I can excuse him."

"But you are going off home sooner than you would have gone if this hadn't happened."

"Perhaps I am, child; but no matter. I'm not angry with Peter, and would do as much for him as if this hadn't happened."

Hannah caught at these words.

"Ah," said she, "Uncle Ben, if you could help him a little!"

Her voice trembled.

"If you could help him a little. He works very hard, and tries to get along. But it's so discouraging to be always under a pressure—to see no light ahead."

Hannah's feelings overcame her, and she leaned her face upon Uncle Ben's shoulder and sobbed violently.

"Don't take on so, child—don't!" said the old man, in a tender, encouraging voice. "Hope for the best. The darkest hour,

UNCLE BEN AND HIS NIECE.

(7)

Pag. 26.

you know, is just before daybreak. I won't forget Peter. Perhaps I can help him. I'll go home and think about it."

"He's very kind to us all, uncle," sobbed Hannah. "And I can't bear to see him so troubled as he is sometimes."

"If he were not quite so set in his ways," replied Uncle Ben—"if he were only a little more ready to learn, it would be a great deal better for all of you."

"I know he's stiff about some things, uncle; but then he means well."

"No doubt of that, Hannah. But, no matter how good a man's intentions are, they will not help him much unless guided by a well-enlightened judgment. And there's lies Peter's defect. But I will see what can be done."

This was enough to inspire Hannah with hope. After the old gentleman had departed, which event took place at the time fixed upon, she meditated on what he had said, and her heart took courage. Uncle Ben was in good circumstances, and fully able to help them, if he would. A few hundred dollars might be spared by him, easily. And how much good a few hundred dollars would do them!

Her hopes were soon whispered in the ears of Peter. At first, he said it was all nonsense to think of any thing from Uncle Ben, and, in the excitement of the moment, called him an old miser. Still Hope did find a lurking-place in his heart, and would not be cast out.

Before the day closed, Peter several times caught himself musing on the vague promise of the old gentleman, and even making some calculations predicated thereon. Since the mortgage on his farm was executed, he had experienced a pressure on his feelings that robbed him of all true peace of mind. Before, he seemed at least to be standing still, if not progressing. Now the first downward step having been taken, final ruin seemed inevitable. A man who feels himself sinking is ready to catch at any thing that promises to bear him above the surface. The act is instinctive, rather than from a determination of the will. Thus it was with Peter; he felt that he was in deep water, and caught at the first straw which floated near him. It was in vain that he reasoned against this hope in his mind, and sought to turn himself from it. Its power over him was not in the least abated by the struggle against it.

At length Peter Miller ceased to search for arguments against the probabilities involved in Hannah's suggestion, and to let his mind rest pleasantly on the certainty of receiving substantial aid from Uncle Ben. Regret for his unhandsome treatment of the old gentleman came with this state, mingled with fear lest he had, in the unreasonableness of his anger, done himself and family a serious injury.

"I shouldn't at all wonder if we heard from Uncle Ben to-morrow," said Hannah, after the children were in bed on New-

Year's Eve, and they sat talking over their future prospects.

Peter shook his head doubtingly, although the expectation of a communication from Uncle Ben was as prominent in his mind as in that of Hannah.

Soon after breakfast, on New-Year's day, Peter, without waiting for a hint from his wife, walked over to the post-office. On his way, spite of all he could do to control his thoughts, they would run on the probable extent of aid to be received from Uncle Ben. The mortgage on the farm was four hundred dollars.

"If he would let us have enough to pay that off"——

He checked himself in the midst of a half-uttered sentence, and called himself a fool for indulging such vain and improbable fancies.

"Any thing for me to-day?" asked Peter of the post-master, on arriving at the office. He almost held his breath with suspense.

"Here's a newspaper for you," replied

the post-master, handing out a small package.

"No letter?" said Peter, while his heart sank heavily.

"None," answered the man.

"Are you sure? Won't you look again?"

Another search was made. The post-master shook his head.

"How much is to pay on this?" asked Peter, as he turned the enveloped paper over and over again in his hands.

"Nothing—the postage is paid," was replied.

Poor Peter Miller, whose feelings had undergone a sudden and painful revulsion, thrust the newspaper into his pocket, and returned slowly homeward.

"Have you been to the post-office?" asked Hannah, as her husband entered the house.

"Yes," was his brief answer.

The gloom on Peter's countenance fell like a shadow on her heart. There was

no need of further question. Hannah felt
this, yet she said—

"Was there nothing for us?"

"No—yes."

And Peter drew the newspaper from his
pocket and commenced tearing off the en-
velope.

"Here's a newspaper, but dear knows
where it came from. Oh! yes!"

He now saw a name written on the margin of the paper—

"Benjamin Hicks."

"Humph! What do I want with his
old newspapers!" And, in the disappointment and anger of the moment, he tossed
the unopened paper into the fire-place.

"Peter!" exclaimed Hannah, springing
forward and snatching the paper from the
fire ere the flames had touched it—"what
are you doing?"

To Hannah's mind had come the quick
suggestion, that a letter, containing money
perhaps, might be enclosed. Hurriedly,

she unfolded it, but there was nothing beyond the large and well-filled newspaper.

"That's an insult which I'll never forgive," said Peter, with much bitterness in
his tone.

"Don't be too hasty, Peter," remarked
Hannah, as she refolded the paper. "Wait
a little while; Uncle Ben is incapable of
deliberately insulting any one."

"He has clearly insulted me; and he
did it deliberately," replied her husband.

"No, no. Don't think so. Uncle Ben
spoke to me very kindly of you. He means
well, but acts strangely sometimes."

"Strange enough! I don't like such well-
meaning men."

And so saying he left the room. As
soon as he was gone, Henry, whose eyes
had been feasting on the newspaper since
the moment his father drew it from his
pocket, seized upon it, and opened it with
a feeling of delight so intense that his very
hands trembled. It was a copy of the
Weekly Cincinnati Gazette, which he im-

mediately commenced reading aloud to his mother and Ellen. About half an hour afterward, Peter Miller returned to the house. Glancing through the window, he saw the paper open in Henry's hands, while his wife and Ellen, who were sewing—though it was New-year's day—were evidently listening with much interest.

Peter was still too angry with Uncle Ben, and felt too great a contempt for his newspaper, to join his family while thus engaged. So he went into the adjoining room. The communicating door stood ajar, and as Peter sat down, he heard distinctly the voice of Henry, as he read to his mother and sister. At first, he tried not to listen; but as the words formed themselves into sentences, his mind took in the thoughts and feelings expressed, and soon, in spite of himself, he became deeply interested. Henry was reading a story of domestic trial, in which a profound trust in Providence sustained the parties introduced, even when their sky was far darker than his had yet been; and when he saw help come to them, in their most painful extremity, and from a point least expected, he could not keep the tears from his eyes. After the story was completed, Henry read for nearly an hour longer, all of which time Peter Miller sat in the adjoining room, listening intently, and equally interested with the others.

All dinner-time, Henry and Ellen talked about what had been read in the "Gazette." They did not know that their father had been as much interested in the contents of the paper as themselves. He remained silent. During the afternoon, as Peter sat in the room with his wife, he picked up the newspaper, which lay temptingly near him—he felt differently toward it, since he had listened to Henry reading from its broad pages—and let his eye glance over it, from column to column.

"Gypsum? gypsum?" said he at length, speaking half to himself, yet looking to-

VII.—3

ward Hannah, as if making inquiry of her.
" What is gypsum?"

" I'm sure I don't know," replied Hannah. " Isn't there a dictionary up-stairs."

" I believe there is, somewhere.   But I
couldn't put my hand on it.   I've not seen
it these five years."

" Let me see," said Hannah thoughtfully;
" where is it? Yes—yes; I think I know."
And laying down her mending, she went
up-stairs.   In a little while she returned
with the book in her hand, open; and as
she entered the room said—" Gypsum is
plaster of Paris."

" Indeed!   Oh, well, that is simple
enough, then."

" What is simple enough?" asked Hannah.

" You know that we lost nearly our
whole crop of grapes, last year, by a kind
of mildew or rot," said Peter. " I calculated,
certainly, on getting at least a hundred and
fifty dollars from that acre of vineyard, just
in full bearing, and I got nothing worth

sending to market. Now, here a man says that he lost his grapes, year before last, in just the same way: and that, after studying about it a long time, he thought that he would gather the leaves that fell in autumn, and put them around the roots of the vine, adding a little gypsum, and see what effect it would have. Last year every vine thus treated had an abundance of healthy fruit: while on the others, the grapes, just as they were about ripening, decayed as before."

"Is it possible! I'd do the same."

"Indeed I will. As soon as the snow clears off, I'll take a man and go through the entire vineyard. If that will save a hundred or two dollars' worth of grapes, it is well worth the trying. If I had only known this last year!"

A week went by, and then another number of the "Gazette" came. When Peter brought it from the post-office and threw it down, Henry uttered an exclamation of pleasure, and catching it up, opened it with

a delighted eagerness, which his father could
not help observing. He immediately commenced reading aloud for his mother. Peter Miller listened, and soon become as
much interested as he had been in the story read in the preceding number.

After supper that evening, Peter took up
the paper, because he could not help doing
so—the very sight of it producing a desire
to know more of what it contained. He was
reading to himself, when he paused, and
looking up, said, thoughtfully—

"Can that really be so?"

"Can what be so?" asked Hannah.

"If what is said in this paper be true,"
replied Peter, "I can pay off my mortgage
in two years."

"What does it say?" inquired Hannah,
looking surprised.

"It says that swamp-muck, treated in a
certain way, makes a fertilizer equal in value, to lands of a certain character, to the
best stable and barnyard composts. If this
really be so, I can, as just said, pay off the

mortgage in two years; for there are thousands of cart-loads of muck in that swamp across the orchard.   There is a little book, it is further stated here, to be had in Cincinnati, called 'The Muck Manual.'   It really seems too good to be true."

The " Muck Manual" was sent for and obtained, and Peter studied it day and night, for a week.   By that time he understood the matter thoroughly, and it was to him like "light ahead."   Already the pressure of gloomy despondency, as he looked into the future, was, to a great extent, removed. If his vineyard, now five years old, produced a good crop next season, it would net the handsome sum of two or three hundred dollars.   Moreover, if the muck compost answered as well as he was inclined to believe that it would, one or two hundred dollars would be made by using it.

Week after week came the " Gazette" by post; but it did not, as at first, bear upon its margin the name of Benjamin Hicks, for the old gentleman, instead of sending his own copy of the paper had ordered it to be mailed to Peter from the office in Cincinnati. No longer, in the mind of the latter, were unpleasant emotions excited when the postmaster handed him out regularly, on Saturdays, the " Gazette." He would have felt no little disappointment had there been any failure of the paper to reach him with its accustomed regularity.

It is wonderful what a change was wrought in the whole family of Peter Miller, in a very short space of time, by the introduction of a newspaper. Its carefully selected stories, ever inculcating some good principle, or awakening the feelings to warmer sympathies; its current history of passing events; its pleasant melange of wit and humour; and its grave lessons of truth to the understanding, and good impulses to the heart; gave aliment to the hungry minds of parents and children, at the same time that it elevated them into a higher, purer, and healthier region.

In Hannah, who aforetimes used to

warble like a bird from morning till night, the sweet voice of music had become dumb. But, ere the spring opened, that voice was occasionally heard again, breaking forth in snatches of old melodies. It sounded strangely familiar and pleasant to Peter, when this happened; and in his heart awoke a thousand dear, responsive echoes.

Peter himself had become a different man, and was looking hopefully forward to the coming summer, when the experiments he was going to enter upon would be tested. The change in Ellen and Henry was quite as apparent. Both became incited to self-improvement, and got their father to procure them books, in which they studied lessons daily, with the regularity of scholars at school. Their hearts being in what they were doing, they improved wonderfully. This fact pleased both their parents, and increased the cheerfulness of feeling into which they were gradually rising.

During the winter, the sheep of Peter Miller were attacked with the distemper from which they had suffered so fatally the year before. Timely communications in the "Gazette" from large wool-growers in Ohio, among whose flocks the disease had likewise appeared, enabled him to apply remedies, till then unheard of in his neighbourhood, and which prevented the loss of a single animal.

When spring opened, Peter employed two extra hands for some weeks in hauling swamp-muck, and in preparing it for certain fields that needed renovation. Had his knowledge of its valuable fertilizing properties been obtained some four or five months earlier than it was, he could have used it to far greater advantage in that year's crop. As it was, he made a saving, by its substitution, of nearly a hundred dollars.

In many things pertaining to agriculture and stock-raising was Peter's mind enlightened during the spring and summer through the columns of the "Gazette." The value of lime on lands of a particular character he never fully understood, until he saw it clearly set forth in an extract from "The American Farmer," and became aware that, by a proper application of the article, he could keep his fields in a good productive condition, at an expense far below that to which he had long been subjected. Here Peter obtained a first glimpse into the mysteries of agricultural chemistry, without a knowledge of which no farmer can work his ground to the best advantage.

Harvest-time came round at last, and Peter Miller had rather more than an average of root and grain crops. He had six hundred bushels of wheat, five hundred bushels of corn, and two hundred bushels of potatoes to sell, besides hay, oats, rye, etc., sufficient to winter his stock. Moreover—whether from the particular treatment of his vineyard, as suggested by the writer in the "Gazette," or not, we will not venture to say—his vintage brought him one hundred and sixty dollars.

Since the time his fields of golden grain nodded ripe for the harvest, Peter had examined, weekly, with much interest, the quotations of prices in the produce-market, as regularly given in the "Gazette;" and when, at last, he called on Gray & Elder to know what they were going to pay him for his wheat and corn, he knew the highest selling-rate to a cent.   Before offering his produce, he obtained his store-bills, and found that they were nearly four hundred dollars.   The fact was, he had started the year with scarcely a dollar to live on, and was thence compelled to go on trust for every thing until another crop could be taken from the ground.   This bill, added to his mortgage, made a debt of eight hundred dollars.   At the prices quoted in the "Gazette," all his wheat, corn, and potatoes would be absorbed, and still over two hundred dollars of the debt remain.   Here was a very important improvement on last year.   Peter had started some four hundred dollars in debt, and now would owe only two hundred after the sale of his crops. And this more favourable state of his affairs was traced in his mind to the New-Year's gift of Uncle Ben, which, when received, had so deeply incensed him against the old gentleman that even yet he was not fully forgiven.

"What are you paying for wheat?" asked Peter, on calling at the store of Gray & Elder, for the purpose of selling his crop.

"Sixty-five cents," was answered.

"Is that the highest?" said Peter.

"Yes."

Peter shook his head, and replied—

"Wheat is quoted in Cincinnati at seventy-five."

"Indeed!" Mr. Gray *looked* surprised. He did not *feel* so, for he knew the price quite as well as the farmer.

"Yes," said Peter, "it is quoted at seventy-five to eighty in my last number of the 'Gazette.'"

"It costs something to get the wheat to market," remarked Mr. Gray.

"I know it does; but not ten cents a bushel. What are you paying for corn?"

Mr. Gray thought for some moments, and then replied—

"Twenty-two cents."

"Too far below the Cincinnati price," said Peter.

"Ah! What is the price there?"

"Thirty cents."

"We can't give that."

"You can do better than twenty-two cents, however; if not, I must find a market in Cincinnati, for both my wheat and corn."

"How much do you want?" asked Mr. Gray.

"I want as near the Cincinnati price as possible. Say seventy-two for my wheat, and twenty-seven or eight for my corn."

"We can't pay prices like those, Mr. Miller. We'd better give up business."

"Let me know the best you will do," said Peter.

The two partners held a long consultation, and finally agreed to offer sixty-eight for the wheat, and twenty-five for the corn. Peter reflected on this for some time and then said—

"I'll take to-night to think over the matter."

With this resolution he went away. That evening the man who held the mortgage on Peter Miller's farm, came over to say that he wanted his money.

"I'll pay you half," said Peter, "as soon as I sell my wheat and corn. But to settle the whole will be impossible this year."

But the man said he must have the whole. Finally, however, he agreed to take half, if it were paid to him immediately.

Fretted by this application, Peter made up his mind to let Gray & Elder have his wheat and corn at their offer, provided they would cash the amount over and above their bills against him. So on the next morning, he started for their store.

On his way he stopped at the post-office and got his number of the "Gazette," which he put into his pocket without unfolding, and continued on his way to Gray & Elder's. Neither of the men happened to be in, and while waiting for them, Peter took out his newspaper and commenced reading. Almost the first paragraph that met his eyes was the following—

"IMPORTANT RISE IN WHEAT.—The news by the last steamer from Europe, which reports a probable failure in the crops, sent wheat suddenly up from seventy-five cents to a dollar. And even at the advanced rates, holders seem little inclined to sell."

The farmer waited no longer for the grain-merchants, but refolding his paper, thrust it into his pocket and went home. He had not been there over fifteen minutes, when a messenger came from Gray & Elder to know if he was going to accept their offer.

"Tell them," replied Peter, "that I cannot take less than a dollar a bushel for my wheat."

The messenger went back, but did not return again. This was as Peter had supposed it would be. During the day, the man who held the mortgage called again. Peter told him of the rise in wheat, and said that if he sold at the advanced rates, he would pay off the whole debt.

. During the following week, Gray & Elder advanced their offer to ninety cents. But the farmer would not sell. The "Gazette" arrived, and showed a continued firmness in the market for wheat, and an advance for corn. Peter also, in glancing hopefully over the broad pages of the paper, cast his eyes upon the advertising columns, and in them saw the names of a number of millers and merchants advertising for wheat and corn, and offering to "pay the highest market prices in cash."

"Now," said Peter Miller to the store-keepers "if you will take my wheat at a dollar, and my corn at thirty-eight, I'll sell. If not, I'll hold on a little longer."

Gray & Elder, after demurring a little, closed the bargain. So, with the wheat and other crops, the store bill was settled, the mortgage paid off, and a balance left with which to begin the new year.

"So much for a newspaper!" said Peter, speaking to himself, as he walked homeward with the cancelled mortgage in his pocket, after paying off the debt which had been hanging over him. "So much for a newspaper! I do believe, if I'd begun taking a paper ten or a dozen years ago, I'd been a rich man to-day. Yes—Uncle Ben was right; I didn't know my business, proud as I was of being thought a good farmer."

So soon as this favourable change in affairs took place, Mr. and Mrs. Miller conferred together about Henry and Ellen. The reading of a newspaper, weekly, for nearly a year, had gradually filled the minds of the former with an entirely new class of ideas.   They now saw in education the only sure way to prosperity and social elevation for their children, and were mutually prepared to make sacrifices for its attainment.   When the mother said—

"I think, Peter, we ought to send Ellen and Henry to school."

The reply was—

"Just my own view.   They must not remain at home a week longer.   Ellen has been sadly neglected."

"Indeed she has.   It troubles me when I think of it."

They were really in earnest in all this. Ellen and Henry were immediately sent to school; and in the place of the former, a young woman was hired to assist Mrs. Miller in her household duties.

During the Christmas holidays, Uncle Ben came over to Salem on a visit, in order to see what effect his New-Year's gift had produced in the family of his nephew and niece.   That there would be a salutary change, if the newspaper were read, he knew,

but he was not prepared to see effects so re-
markable as were presented. On arriving
at the farm-house—he came unheralded—
he was struck with the air of greater thrift
and comfort that was presented in the external appearance of things. No one observing his approach, he walked up as far
as the door, and was about opening it, when
he paused to listen to the voice of Hannah;
she was singing one of the old pleasant
songs he had heard her warble so often when
she was the happy inmate of his own house,
and there was as much heart—so to speak—
in her voice as in days of yore. The old man
listened for a few moments, and then lift-
ing the latch, stepped into the room, taking
all its inmates by surprise. Miller sat with
the newspaper in his hand, so intent upon
what he was reading, that he did not perceive that any one had entered the room.
Hannah stood at the ironing-table, and
Ellen, tidily dressed, and looking so changed in every thing, that Uncle Ben hardly
recognised her, was sewing; while Henry

sat as much engaged with a book as his father was with the newspaper.

"Uncle Ben!" exclaimed Hannah in a glad voice—she was the first to observe his entrance.

Instantly Peter Miller was on his feet, and approaching the old man, grasped his hand tightly.

"You have forgiven me, then, for saying you were not a good farmer! Ha! my boy?" said the old gentleman, laughing, as he returned Peter's hearty shake.

"Yes—yes, a thousand times over."

"And I was right, was I not?"

"Undoubtedly you were—undoubtedly."

"That's the 'Gazette' I see in your hand. Do you read it?"

"Yes, every line."

"And it's been of use to you?"

"Of use! I guess it has. It's paid off the mortgage, and left me something over."

"Hardly done so much as that, Peter?" replied the old gentleman incredulously.

"I tell you it has, Uncle Ben. Why, I

would not be without the paper for a hundred dollars a year!"

The meaning of all this was explained to Uncle Ben with great particularity during the next hour.

"It's all turned out in the way I hoped, only a great deal better," said he, when Peter had given him a full history of his year's experience. "I was going to lend you enough money to pay off your mortgage; but, judging from what I saw and heard at my last visit, I concluded that it would do no real good. In a year or two, going on as you were, all would be involved again, and my money lost. You worked hard, so did Hannah, and so did every body around you, but it was work without wisdom, and such work never turns out well. It is like rowing with a single oar in the teeth of a strong current. What was wanted I saw at a glance, and I determined to supply the want. A man who doesn't take and read the newspapers, and yet expects to succeed as a farmer, is not much wiser than the sailor who puts to sea without chart or compass, and will be as likely to reach the ultimate haven of success."

And Uncle Ben was right.

D 2

THE TEMPERANCE TRACT.

A YOUNG man, who felt a good deal of enthusiasm in the temperance cause, procured some tracts for distribution. He had a dozen, and in the ardour of his feelings he calculated that at least twelve men would be reformed through their agency. Having an idle afternoon to devote to the cause, he started out with his dozen tracts in his pocket, his mind in some degree of elation in prospect of the good that was to be done.

In walking along, the first man who came in his way was a tavern-keeper.

" Here is a good subject," said Wilton to himself, as the tavern-keeper drew near.

THE TEMPERANCE TRACT.

Page 64

"Let me see what I have that will suit him. Ah! this is it. 'An Appeal to the People on the Liquor Traffic.'"

And, selecting a tract with this title, he presented it to the tavern-keeper as they met, saying, as he did so—

"Accept this, if you please."

Taken by surprise, the man received the tract, and the distributor, bowing, moved on.

"A dead shot for him!" thought he; but the thought was scarcely formed ere he felt a hand laid roughly upon his shoulder. Turning quickly, he confronted the tavern-keeper, whose face was red with anger.

"What's this?" he demanded imperatively.

"Its a tract," replied the young man, looking confused.

"See here, my friend!" and as the tavern-keeper spoke he withdrew his hand from his shoulder. "My first impulse was to pitch you over that fence. On second thoughts, however, I will let you go unpunished for your impertinence; but, with this piece of good advice—If you wish to keep out of trouble, mind your own business."

Then crumpling the tract in his hand, and tossing it from him contemptuously, he turned away, leaving the young temperance reformer with his enthusiasm in the cause down to zero. While this state of mind was predominant, the balance of the tracts on hand was thrown over a fence, and, meeting a gust of wind, were scattered apart and driven in various directions. The distributor returned home feeling mortified and discouraged. On reflection, however, he was vexed at himself, both for the bungling manner in which he had proceeded, and for his having been so easily thrown off by a rebuff.

" The tracts, at least, needn't have been wasted," said he; "that was a folly of which I ought to be heartily ashamed."

About an hour after this occurrence, a man came walking along the road, near where this little adventure took place. A piece of paper caught his eye, and, stooping, he picked it up. Moving on as he opened it, he commenced reading, and was soon deeply interested, for he walked slower and slower, and sometimes stopped altogether. This man was also a tavern-keeper. After reading the tract through, he placed it in his pocket, and continued on his way.

"Stop and think, John," said a wife, in an appealing voice to her husband, as the latter was about leaving the house.

"Don't talk to me in that way!" replied the husband impatiently. "You couldn't act worse, if I were a common drunkard."

"But the danger, John. Stop and think of that! There is a lion in your way."

"I am out of all patience with you, Alice," said the man. "A high respect you have for your husband's good sense and good principles! As if I couldn't enjoy a glass now and then, without being in danger of becoming a miserable sot."

With this, the man turned off, and took his way to the tavern, while his wife went weeping into the house. As he walked along, the words she had uttered—"Stop and think"—rang in his ears, and he tried to push them from his thoughts in order that he might not think. All at once, a fresh blast of wind blew from a field that adjoined the road a piece of paper, and as it fell at his feet his eyes caught the words—

"STOP AND THINK."

The coincidence of language startled him for a moment. He took up the piece of paper and commenced reading; and as he read, he walked slower and slower. One of Wilton's temperance tracts had fallen into his hands. It was a close appeal to the moderate drinker, and set forth his danger in the fullest manner. At last the man stood still. Then he sat down by the roadside, still reading on.

"There is danger," he at length murmured, folding up the tract as he spoke

Rising, he stood resolute as to whether he should return home, or keep on his way to the tavern. Had any one thrust the tract into his hand, he would have rejected it; but coming to him as it did, it found his mind prepared to hearken to its appeals. But the love of drink had been formed, and, at the prospect of having its accustomed gratification cut of, began to cry out for indulgence. A combat in the mind of the man was the result; and this continued until appetite gained the victory so far, that he concluded, for this time at least, to go to the tavern, but to give up the habit thereafter.

"I hate to turn back after I once start to do a thing," said he, as he moved on again toward the tavern. "It's bad luck."

Still the argument for and against any further indulgence kept going on; and he could not turn his mind away from it.

At length the sign of the "Punch Bowl," whither he was wending his way, came in view; and the sight affected him with the old pleasure. In imagination, the refreshing and exhilarating glass was at his lips, and he quickened his pace involuntarily.

As he drew near, he saw the landlord sitting in the porch. The good-natured old fellow did not smile with the broad smile of welcome that usually played over his countenance when a customer approached.

"How are you to-day, landlord?" said the man cheerfully, as he stepped upon the porch.

"Do you know what road you have come?" asked the landlord with a gravity of manner that surprised his customer.

"Yes," replied the man; "I came the road to the 'Punch Bowl.'"

"Better say the road to ruin," returned the landlord.

"What's the matter?" inquired the man. "I never heard a landlord talk in that way before."

"It was the road to ruin to poor Bill

Jenkins. That I know too well; and has been the road to ruin of a good many more that I don't like to think about. It will be your road to ruin if you keep on; so I would advise you to stop and think a little on the matter. If you want any liquor, you can get it from Jim at the bar; but I'd rather not have your sixpence in my till to-day. I won't feel right about it."

" What's the matter, landlord? What has put you in this humour?" said the man; who, in turn, became serious.

" I found a piece of paper on the road as I walked along just now, and it had something printed on it that has set me to thinking. That's the matter. Ah me! I wish I was in a better business. It doesn't make a man feel very pleasant to think that in building himself up he has dragged others down. And I'm rather afraid that's my position. So go home, my friend, and don't let the sin of your ruin be on my conscience. You've got to loving liquor a little too well. May be you don't think so; but I know it.   I've seen a great many men go down the hill, and I can tell the first steps.   You have taken them.   Stop and think before you go any farther."

"Look here, landlord," said the man, after standing thoughtful for a few minutes, "I'll make a bargain with you."

"Very well, what about?"

"If you'll quit selling, I'll quit drinking."

The landlord did not answer for some moments, but sat with his eyes upon the floor.   At length, rising up slowly, he extended his hand to his customer, and grasping it firmly he said—

"Agreed! it's a bargain!"

A hearty shake sealed the contract.

An hour afterward, those who went by the "Punch Bowl" saw the bar closed; and in less than an hour afterward, the sad-hearted wife, who had seen her husband walking in the road to ruin, saw him return as sober as when he left; and heard with gladness his promise never again to put the cup of confusion to his lips.

Thus it is that truth, scattered even in the fields and by the roadside, finds its way into the minds of men, and does its work on their hearts. Our most imperfect and defective efforts are often overruled by Providence to the accomplishment of the greatest good.

FALSE FRIENDS AND TRUE.

"YOU do not seem happy, Julia," said Mrs. Hartly to her daughter, who, half an hour before, had come home from a visit to one of her young friends. "Nothing unpleasant has occurred, I hope."

"I wish I could say no," replied Julia, looking into her mother's face, while a crimson glow overspread her own. "But I cannot."

"I am sorry to hear you speak thus, Julia. I hope your friend Anna has not given you cause for painful feelings."

"Indeed she has, ma! I never could have believed it, but she spoke to me this afternoon in a cruel way, and Julia burst into tears, and continued to sob for some moments.

"I am grieved at this," said Mrs. Hartly; after her daughter's excitement had in a measure subsided. "But I am sure from what I have seen of Anna, that there must have occurred some strange misunderstanding between you, or she never could have uttered a word to give you pain. Tell me what she said to you, and why she said it."

"We were talking about the party to be given by Mary Williams, next week," Julia replied, "and differed about some trifle, too unimportant to mention, when Anna got angry because I could not agree with her, and said I was always obstinate, and fond of disagreeing. If any one else had said so to me, I would not have cared so much; but for Anna Miller to talk so to my face, was too bad!"

"But Anna is no doubt sorry for what she said. Certainly she apologized on the instant, for her unkind remark."

"I didn't give her a chance," said Julia indignantly, "for I picked up my bonnet, and was out of the house in two minutes."

"There you were wrong, my daughter. Hasty and impulsive actions are hardly ever such as reason, in sober moods, would dictate. When Anna spoke as she did, she was, in a certain sense, beside herself, and did not utter her true sentiments in regard to you. You should, in justice to yourself and her too, have given her the opportunity of recalling her unkind words. And that she would have done so, I have not the least doubt."

"But even if she had," urged Julia, "it would have altered the case but little. If there had not existed in her mind previously, the thought which she uttered, it would not have been clothed in words while she was under excitement. And I have no notion of being on terms of intimacy with any one who thinks me obstinate and fond of disagreeing with everybody."

"If such an idea really exists in her mind, Julia, I doubt if it could have found a place there, unless something in your character had caused her, even against her will, to give it a place. This being so, is it not much worse for you to have a fault, than for her to perceive it, involuntarily?"

"But I don't think I am obstinate, or fond of disagreeing with every one."

"As to that, Julia," said Mrs. Hartly, "you are rather too much given to expressing differences of opinion, where there is no use in appearing to differ. Your father and myself have both noticed this peculiarity in your disposition, and regretted it."

Julia coloured deeply, and hung down her head in silence. But her state of indignation against Anna Miller, prevented her from seeing clearly the fault pointed out by her mother.

About the same time that the brief conversation, just referred to, took place between Mrs. Hartly and her daughter, Anna

Miller sat weeping bitterly, in her own chamber. She was a kind-hearted girl, and loved, with a true affection, the young friend she had, in a moment of excitement, so deeply offended. But she was not blind to Julia's faults, though always disposed to excuse them, notwithstanding she was not unfrequently annoyed by her too evident inclination to differ in opinion about the merest trifle, and not only to differ, but to make the difference of importance.

While thus indulging the grief of an affectionate heart, an elder sister came in, and seeing her distress, said—

" Why, Anna, what does ail you ?"

Anna looked up, and after a moment's hesitation, replied—

" Why, sister, I have let my hasty temper get the mastery over me, so far as to talk very unkindly to Julia Hartly, and she has gone home deeply offended."

" I am sorry for that, Anna. But what did you say to her ?"

" We differed about some trifle, and she,

as is usual, you know, with her, made a matter of considerable importance out of the difference. Somehow or other, I felt irritated at this, and said to her, more sharply I presume than I intended, 'Julia, you are strangely obstinate, always differing with some one!' At this she picked up her bonnet, and was out of the house before I had time to apologize."

"Well, Anna, I am sorry for you; but it cannot be recalled now. You must profit by this lesson, painful as it is, and endeavour to exercise more control over yourself, as well as forbearance toward others. When you next see Julia, you can explain it all; and there, I hope, the unpleasant part of the affair will end."

"I must see her in the course of tomorrow, apologize, and have the whole affair settled; for Mary Williams's party takes place on the next evening, and we must be on good terms again by that time, or there will be no enjoyment for me."

"A good resolution, Anna," said her

sister. "Seek an explanation, and reconciliation, as soon as possible, and all will be well again."

Shortly after Julia Hartly had explained to her mother the cause of her unhappiness, Emeline West, a mutual acquaintance of Julia and Anna, called in, and the two young ladies soon retired to Julia's chamber, to talk about certain matters and things which are not considered appropriate themes for discussion in the presence of mothers.

"Oh, Emeline!" said Julia, after the door had been closed upon them, "I've been treated most shamefully to-day, by Anna Miller."

"You don't say so, Julia! How in the world did that happen?"

"I wouldn't have believed it was in her to say to me what she did! We were talking about Mary Williams's party, when I differed with her about the length of a flounce, and gave her my reason for it. At this, she flew into such a passion, and said that I was an obstinate girl, and was always differing with some one."

" It isn't possible !"

" Indeed it is, then! I never was so hurt in my life," said Julia.

" And what did you do?" asked her young friend.

" Why, I put on my bonnet, and was out of the house in a twinkling."

" That was right! I like to see every one act with becoming spirit."

"She's mistaken, I can tell her, if she thinks to trifle with me in that way! I never take an insult, tamely, from any one," responded Julia, excited and indignant.

" I always knew her to be a passionate and insulting girl. This is not the first instance, by half a dozen, that I have heard of her outrageous violations of ladylike deportment toward her friends,—and in her own house, too !"

" Well, she'll never have a chance of insulting me again, I can tell her!" said

Julia, feeling more and more indignant, as the "mutual friend" went on to widen, instead of endeavouring to heal the breach that had been made between two, who had really been fond of each other.

"You would be a fool if you did," Emeline replied significantly; "I, for one, have no idea of tolerating these constantly recurring violations of good breeding and good feeling. If we allow them to pass unnoticed, or forgive them as soon as perpetrated, we will soon have a pretty state of things. No one, after a while, will feel free from the danger of insult in any company. For one, I have long since resolved to set my face against them; and I am glad to find that you have shown a proper spirit of resentment toward Anna Miller; who is, any how, to say the least of it, a vulgar and forward girl."

In this way the "mutual friend" went on to confirm Julia's unkind feelings toward Anna, and thus to extinguish the hope that had already begun to spring up in her mind, that she would seek an explanation.

On that same evening Emeline West called to see Anna Miller.

"You look serious, Anna," said she, after they were alone.

"Do I? Well, I must confess that I feel a little sober," Anna replied, endeavouring to smile.

"What is the matter? Has any thing happened?"

"Nothing of much consequence," said Anna, evasively.

"I saw Julia Hartly this afternoon," Emeline remarked, after a pause.

"Did you, indeed!" said Anna, in a quicker tone.

"Yes, and she seems to be in rather a queer way. What has happened, for she was as tart as a damson when I mentioned your name."

"I was rather rude to her this afternoon," replied Anna, "but she went away before I had time to explain myself and apologize."

"She is a touchy kind of girl, any way."

"I don't know," said Anna Miller; "I have sometimes talked very plainly to her without giving offence. But, to-day, I gave her just cause for being displeased. I only regret that I did not prevent her from going away, until after I had asked forgiveness for what I had said."

"I don't think it would have been of any use," returned Emeline. "She says that you insulted her, downright, in your own house, and that she is determined to set her face against all such unlady-like conduct in any one. I told her that she must forgive if she expected to be forgiven; but she said that if she did forgive, she would never forget; and that, anyhow, she would not forgive you, until she had punished you well for having so grossly insulted her."

Anna's face coloured deeply, and her eyes became suffused with tears. But she made no reply. Ever since Julia had left the house, she had been pondering over various forms of reconciliation, and had fully made up her mind, that early in the morning she would call upon Julia, and seek to heal the wounds she had made; but the information given by Emeline, of Julia's state of feeling, dispersed at once her fond anticipations, and aroused in her mind something of resentment toward her estranged friend.

"What was the mighty offence, Anna?" inquired her visitor, affecting ignorance of what had passed between the two young ladies.

"There is no denying, Emeline, that I was a little rude to her," said Anna, "for I made so free as to tell her that she was an obstinate girl."

"Well, and so she is. But, in the name of goodness! was that all the wonderful insult she is so full of indignation about? Upon my word!"

"Yes, that is all; and, to tell the truth,

that constant differing with you in any opinion or preference, which she indulges, is, to say the least of it, very annoying."

"Indeed it is! Many a time has she worried me so, that I could hardly keep from telling her a piece of my mind in right plain terms."

"I did intend," remarked Anna, "to go and see her to-morrow morning, and offer an acknowledgment for what I had done. But if she thinks and talks as you say, I'm afraid there will be no use in it."

"I'm sure that there would not be a particle of use in it. And, since she chooses to make such a mountain out of a molehill, if I were you, I would let her have her own way about it."

"Still," said Anna, "Julia has many good qualities, and I always was fond of her. How foolish it was in me, to suffer my impatient temper to cause a separation! This breach must yet be healed; and I am satisfied that I ought to make the first advances."

"You must, of course, judge in the matter for yourself," replied Emeline, tossing her head, "but I make it a point never to humour folks that cut up such tantrums with me. She knew well enough that you spoke hastily, and as she provoked you to speak so, it was for her to consider your peculiarities of character, as much as it is for you to consider her's. Anyhow, she didn't show off so very well, thus to huff up in a minute, and flirt away before you had time to say a word. I wouldn't take all the blame to myself, if I were you. It's a maxim, you know, that where two have a falling out, that one is generally as much in fault as the other; and I am sure, I can't see why you should vary the adage to your own disadvantage."

Thus the mutual friend of the young ladies, from the strange pleasure she took in seeing others at variance, extinguished in the mind of Anna the determination she had formed of going, on the next morning, to seek a reconciliation with her friend.

The night for the party at Mary Williams's came round, and yet Julia and Anna had not seen each other, and each was oppressed with painful feelings, when the idea of meeting at the party presented itself.

"I really feel like staying away," said Anna to her sister; "I know that I shall not enjoy myself, and my presence there must modify, in a good degree, Julia's satisfaction."

"But why not, even there, offer her a friendly hand, and ask to be forgiven for your unkindness toward her. No one need understand what you are saying to her. I am sure that she will gladly respond to your offer of reconciliation."

"I should have done this before now, had I not learned from Emeline West, that she was so much incensed against me."

"Emeline acted very wrong in telling you."

"That may be, sister; but now that I know her real feelings, how can I go forward, under the certainty of being repulsed and wounded."

"Such a certainty, I am sure, does not exist; the worst person can hardly repulse one who comes confessing a wrong, much less a girl who has the many amiable qualities possessed by Julia."

"But you know what she said to Emeline."

"Yes; and I know, too, how easy it is to convey an erroneous impression of what another has said. The very tone of voice and expression of countenance used in repeating any thing, may so modify it as to make it seem very different from what was intended to be conveyed, when it was uttered."

Anna was silenced, but not convinced. The idea that Julia intended, if she forgave her at all, to keep back the forgiveness for some time, in order to punish her, wounded her pride a good deal, and she could not get it out of her mind, nor subdue its influence over her. It seemed so cruel, and so much like trifling with the feelings of one who had loved her, and who still, she must know, entertained for her much true affection.

Anna Miller was among the latest who came to Mary Williams's party that evening. She did not observe Julia when she entered the brilliantly-lighted room. But that young lady saw her, of course, and so did their mutual friend, Miss West, who sat beside Julia.

"She didn't even look at you!" whispered Emeline.

Julia did not reply, but a deep and oppressive sigh struggled up from her bosom, yet without affording her any relief from a weight that seemed bearing down both mind and body.

"She has a guilty look, hasn't she?" again whispered Emeline, as Anna, on taking a chair, turned toward Julia. The latter dropped her eyes beneath those of her estranged friend, while she felt the blood rising into and burning on her cheek.

Even in the brief, flitting glance she had of Anna's face, she saw in its expression that which drew her toward her, and made her heart ache for the estrangement that kept them asunder. It was any thing but a guilty face. But there was in it something of tenderness and sadness, and the reflection of a heart that yearned toward her friend.

"I wonder if she will speak to you?" Emeline again said, breaking into the thoughts of peace that were crowding upon the mind of Julia.

"I don't know, but I am resolved to speak to her," said Julia.

"Don't do that for the world!" returned Emeline, looking Julia in the face with an expression of surprise upon her countenance. "It's her place to make advances toward you: and, if you were to speak to her, from what I heard her say, I am sure she would pass you with contempt. You will not, certainly, run the risk of being so mortified before the whole company."

VII.—6

Thus urged, the hastily formed good resolution was dismissed, and Julia determined to await, in painful suspense, the accidents of the evening, hoping that something would occur to break down the partition that separated them. Her very heart yearned within her to be reconciled. She loved Anna, had forgiven her hasty words, and now only wanted an opportunity to tell her so. And had not their officious mutual friend interposed her unkindly offices, the breach would have been healed, through overtures from Julia, before the evening of the day after the offence had been received.

It was not long after Anna entered the room, before Emeline managed to get along side of her.

"You have not made that little matter up I see," she remarked, after chatting for a few minutes, glancing at the same time toward Julia, who, on being invited, had taken her seat at the piano.

"No, but I hope we soon will;" was Anna's prompt reply.

"It is to be hoped so," the mutual friend said dryly.

Just then Julia's fingers fell lightly upon the keys of the instrument. She had a sweet voice, and Anna always loved to hear her sing. She now listened with interest. The first line, warbled in pensive sweetness, drew the tears to her eyes, and it was only by an effort that she could keep down her feelings as the song progressed. It was the following:

> "We have been friends together,
>   In sunshine and in shade,
>   Since first beneath the chestnut-trees
>   In infancy we play'd.
>   But coldness dwells within thy heart,
>   A cloud is on thy brow;
>   We have been friends together—
>   Shall a light word part us now?
>
> "We have been gay together;
>   We have laugh'd at little jests,
>   For the fount of hope was gushing
>   Warm and joyous in our breasts.
>   But laughter now hath fled thy lip,

And sullen glooms thy brow;
We have been gay together—
   Shall a light word part us now?

"We have been.sad together;
   We have wept with bitter tears
O'er the grass-grown graves where slumber'd
   The hopes of early years.
The voices which were silent there
   Would bid thee clear thy brow;
We have been *sad* together—
   Oh! what shall part us now?"

"Beautiful!—beautiful!" "Tender!" "Touching!" "Sweet!" were the gratified expressions that ran round the room, as Julia's voice trembled sweetly, and with emphatic tenderness, on the last line. A half-stifled sob which escaped the lips of Anna, attested the influence of the words just sung, upon her feelings.

"She is still the same, affectionate, warm-hearted girl!" she mentally exclaimed.

"Did you ever see a finer piece of tri

fling than that in your life?" said Emeline West to Anna.

"Trifling, Emeline?"

"Certainly! I hope you don't think there is any thing sincere in all that. No —no—it's a precious piece of acting! If she really felt the sentiments of the song just sung, she would never expose them here. She could not."

There was the semblance of truth in what Emeline said, and this clouded and confused Anna's mind. Doubts again arose, and the impulse she felt to go up to Julia and whisper in her ear, as she sat on the piano-stool turning over the music-book, "A light word *shall* *not* part us," was allowed to subside. She now felt more unhappy than ever.

During the evening the two estranged friends were frequently thrown so together, that a word, if only uttered, would have healed the rankling wound. But whenever there was an opportunity, their evil genius seemed to know it; for Emeline was always prompt to drop a warning word, or draw an uncharitable inference, and thus prevent a reconciliation. Anna retired at an early hour, and, after she was gone, Julia felt but little inclination to stay; for while Anna was present, she could not help feeling, constantly, the hope that she would speak to her, and then all would have been forgiven on the instant.

She was sitting alone, gloomily, about half an hour after Anna had left, pondering upon the painful state of estrangement that existed between her and her friend, when a lady sat down by her side and said kindly—

"You do not seem happy, Julia?"

Julia started, and looked into the face of the person who had addressed her, with a momentary expression of surprise, and then replied, while a faint smile lit up her face—

"I cannot say that I do feel very happy, Mrs. Moreland."

"But you need not feel so, Julia. I have just learned from Emeline West that

there is a difficulty between you and Anna
Miller. I know the reason, now, why
neither of you seemed as lively as usual to-
night. Both of you are distressed about
the same cause. Now, surely, you can
forgive each other."

"I do forgive her with all my heart,
Mrs. Moreland," said Julia, the tears filling
her eyes.

"Then I know that forgiveness will be
mutual."

"I fear not," returned Julia. "Emeline
West tells me that Anna thinks and speaks
very unkindly of me. If it had not been
for this, I should have gone to her before
now."

"To say the least of it, then, Emeline is
very much to blame for telling you so,"
said Mrs. Moreland gravely.

"That may be true enough, as far as she
is concerned; but having heard as much,
how can I run the risk of being repulsed?
That would wound me more than the first
offence."

"I am sure, Julia, there is no danger," Mrs. Moreland said encouragingly.

"I could hope not; yet I fear to run any risk. And, besides, the offence was against me, and committed by Anna in her own house. It is for her to come to me."

"And you will not repulse her?"

"Repulse her! Oh no! I could not do that, Mrs. Moreland! I would be the happiest creature in the world, if she would only come and say, 'Julia, let us be friends again.'"

On the next morning, Mrs. Moreland went early to see Anna Miller.

"Well, Anna, how were you pleased last night?" asked the visitor, after a few remarks succeeding the salutations of the morning had passed.

"It was a very pleasant company, Mrs. Moreland."

"But you didn't seem happy, I thought, Anna; and I have taken the liberty of a friend to call on you this morning, in the hope that I can say something, or do something, to make you feel pleasanter."

Anna looked up into the face of her kind friend, with something of surprise in her countenance; and after a few moments' silence, said—

"When we are conscious of having acted wrong, we can find but little external comfort."

"That is true, Anna, in one sense. But if a friend can aid us in correcting what is wrong, then a friend can help us much, even under such circumstances."

"I should be glad to receive any aid, even in that way, Mrs. Moreland. But do you know the cause of my unhappiness?"

"I think I do, Anna."

"Well, what shall I do?"

"I think you ought to go and see Julia."

"I am afraid she will not receive me kindly."

"I am sure she will, Anna!"

"But Emeline West told me that Julia had resolved to keep me at a distance, for the purpose of punishing me for my offence against her."

"It is very strange, Anna, that Emeline West should be as ready to prejudice the mind of Julia against you, as she seems to have been to prejudice your mind against Julia!"

"Surely, Mrs. Moreland, she has not acted thus!"

"I do not like to censure any one, but I am afraid that she has."

"Can it be possible! But do you think Julia would receive me kindly?"

"Anna, I know that she would. I have conversed with her, and she told me, with the tears in her eyes, that if you would only come to see her, she would be the happiest creature in the world."

"Did she, indeed, say that, Mrs. Moreland?" Anna asked eagerly, catching hold of that lady's hands and clasping them in her own.

"Yes, Anna, she did; and she meant all that she said."

"Then I will see her before another hour passes over my head."

"Do so, Anna, and all will again be well," said Mrs. Moreland kindly.

"But will you not go with me?" asked Anna.

"Certainly, if you wish me."

· Then I will see her at once."

On that morning, soon after the break-fast-hour, Emeline West dropped in to see Julia Hartly.

"Ah, good morning, Julia! How do you do after last night's party?" said that young lady in a sprightly tone.

"Pretty well, Emeline; how are you?"

"Oh, lively! I'm glad to see you brightening up a little. You looked too sad and wo-begone, last night, for any thing."

"I did not feel very happy then, Emeline, and I cannot say that I am in very extraordinary spirits this morning. But as I have some hope of a reconciliation with Anna, I cannot but feel a little better than I did then."

"You are not going to humble yourself to her, I hope?"

"No."

"Then she is not going to do it to you, I know! Catch her doing such a thing!"

"I don't wish her to," replied Julia.

"She can't make the first advances without stooping," said Emeline.

Before Julia had time to reply, the parlour-door opened, and Anna, accompanied by Mrs. Moreland, entered.

The two friends looked at each other for a brief moment, and then, without uttering a word, rushed into each other's arms.

"Am I forgiven, Julia?" said Anna, at length.

"Oh yes, a thousand times!" Julia responded warmly.

"And may no hasty word ever again separate you," said Mrs. Moreland. "But should such an event again occur, I sincerely hope our friend Emeline, here, will exercise her influence as a mutual friend, with more discretion and kindness. Had

she acted a true part, your estrangement,
I am convinced, could not have continued
up to this time, short as the period is; and
how much pain you would both have been
spared, I need not say."

Emeline looked surprised and rebuked
for a moment, and then hung down her
head, while her face was crimsoned with
burning blushes of shame. Then suddenly
rising, she hastily retired.

"And now, my young friends," said Mrs.
Moreland, "beware of uttering an unkind
or hasty word. But should either of you
again fall into temptation, let not the sun
go down upon your anger; and above all,
do not listen for a moment to any one who
shows a disposition to widen the breach.
Hearken, rather, to the voice that pleads
for reconciliation; it is the voice of truth
and nature. And, moreover, let the causes
that produced this temporary alienation be
searched out and put away; causes there
must be for it, existing, too, in the minds
of both. Remove these, and you remove

the danger of any future misunderstandings, and disarm evil minds and evil tongues from all power to hurt you. Thus will you be enabled to extract good from what seemed a most painful occurrence. As for Emeline, she is one of a very large class. Some act with more address and caution than she has acted, but the 'poison of adders' is under their tongues. Beware of them!"

HEARTS MADE GLAD

Page 116

CHRISTMAS PRESENTS.

A STORY FOR THE HOLIDAYS.

"DIDN'T he make you a present of any thing, Lizzy?" asked Margaret Granger of her cousin, Lizzy Green.

"No, not even of a strawberry cushion," spoke up Lizzy's sister Jane, "which he could have bought for a sixpence. I think he's a selfish, stingy fellow, so I do; and if he doesn't keep Lizzy on bread and water when he gets her, my name is not Jane Green."

"I wouldn't have him," said Margaret, jestingly, yet half in earnest. "Let Christmas go by and not make his sweetheart or sister a present of the most trifling value!

He must have a penny soul. Why, Harry Lee sent me the 'Leaflets of Memory' and a pair of the sweetest flower-vases you ever saw, and he only comes to see me as a friend. And Cousin William made me a present of a splendid copy of 'Mrs. Hall's Sketches,' the most interesting book I ever read. Besides, I received lots of things. Why, my table is full of presents."

"You have been quite fortunate," said Lizzy, in a quiet voice; "much more so than Jane and I, if to receive a great many Christmas presents is to be considered fortunate."

"But don't you think Edward might have sent you some token of good-will and affection in this holiday season, when every one is giving or receiving presents?" asked Margaret.

"Nothing of the kind was needed, Cousin Maggy, as an expression of his feelings toward me," replied Lizzy. "He knew that I understood their true quality, and felt that any present would have been a useless formality."

"You can't say the same in regard to Jane. He might have passed her the usual compliments of the season."

"Certainly he might," said Jane. "Lizzy needn't try to excuse him after this lame fashion. Of course, there is no cause for the omission but meanness—that's my opinion, and I speak it out boldly."

"It isn't right to say that, sister," remarked Lizzy. "Edward has other reasons for omitting the prevalent custom at this season—and good reasons, I am well assured. As to the charge of meanness, I don't think the fact you allege a sufficient ground for making it."

"Well, I do, then," said Cousin Margaret. "Why, if I were a young man and engaged in marriage to a lady, I'd sell my shoes but what I'd give her something as a Christmas present."

"Yes—or borrow or beg the money," chimed in Jane.

"Every one must do as he or she thinks best," replied Lizzy. "As for me, I am content without a holiday gift, being well satisfied that meanness on the part of Edward has nothing to do with it."

But notwithstanding Lizzy said this, she could not help feeling a little disappointed —more, perhaps, on account of the appearance of the thing than from any suspicion that meanness had any thing to do with the omission.

"I wish Edward had made Lizzy some kind of a present," said Mrs. Green to her husband a day or two after the holiday had passed; "if it had only been for the looks of the thing. Jane has been teasing her about it ever since, and calls it nothing but meanness in Edward. And I'm afraid he is a little close."

"Better that he should be so than too free," replied Mr. Green; "though I must confess that a dollar or two, or even ten dollars, spent at Christmas in a present for his intended bride, could hardly have been set down to the score of prodigality. It does look mean, certainly."

"He is doing very well."

"He gets a salary of eight hundred dollars, and I suppose it doesn't cost him over four or five hundred dollars to live—at least it ought not to do so."

"He has bought himself a snug little house, I am told."

"If he's done that, he's done very well," said Mr. Green; and I can forgive him for not spending his money in Christmas presents, that are never of much use, say the best you will of them. I'd rather Edward would have a comfortable house to put his wife in than see him loading her down before marriage, with presents of one foolish thing and another."

"True. But he should have given the girl something, if it had only been a book, a purse, or some such trifle."

"For which trifles he would have been as strongly charged with meanness as he is

now.   Better let it go as it is.   No doubt
he has good reasons for his conduct."

Thus Mr. Green and Lizzy defended
Edward, while the mother and Jane scold-
ed about his meanness.

Edward Mayfield, of whom these things
were said, was a young man of good principles, prudent habits, and really generous
feelings; but his generosity did not con-
sist in wasting his earnings in order that
he might be thought liberal and open-hand-
ed, but in doing real acts of kindness where
he saw that kindness was needed.   He had
saved from his salary, in the course of four
or five years, enough to buy himself a very
snug house, and had a few hundred dollars
in the Savings' Bank with which to furnish
it when the time came for him to get mar-
ried.   This time was not very far off when
the Christmas, to which allusion has been
made, came round.   At this holiday season, Edward had intended to make both
Lizzy and her sister a handsome present,
and he had been thinking for some weeks

as to what it should be. Many articles, both useful and merely ornamental, were thought of, but none of them exactly pleased his fancy.

A day or two before Christmas, he sat thinking about the matter, when something or other gave a new turn to his reflections.

"They don't really need any thing," said he to himself, "and yet I propose to spend twenty dollars in presents merely for appearance' sake. Is this right?"

"Right, if you choose to do it," he replied to himself.

"I am not so sure of that," he added, after a pause. And then he sat in quite a musing mood for some minutes.

"That's better," he at length said, rising up and walking about the floor. "That would be money and good feeling spent to a better purpose."

"But they'll expect something," he argued with himself; "the family will think so strangely of it. Perhaps I'd better spend half the amount in elegant books for Lizzy and Jane, and let the other go in the way I propose."

This suggestion, however, did not satisfy him.

"Better let it all go in the other direction," he said, after thinking awhile longer; "it will effect a real good. The time will come when I can explain the whole matter, if necessary, and do away with any little false impression that may have been formed."

To the conclusion at which Edward arrived, he remained firm. No present of any kind was made to his betrothed or her sister, and the reader has seen in what light the omission was viewed.

Christmas-eve proved to be one of unusual inclemency. The snow had been falling all day, driven into every nook and corner, cleft and cranny, by a piercing north-easter; and now, although the wind had ceased to roar among the chimneys and to whirl the snow with blinding violence into the face of any one who ventured abroad, the broad flakes were falling slowly but more heavily than since morning, though the ground was covered already to the depth of many inches. It was a night to make the poor feel sober as they gathered more closely around their small fires, and thought of the few sticks of wood or pecks of coal that yet remained of their limited store.

On this dreary night, a small boy, who had been at work in a printing-office all day, stood near the desk of his employer, waiting to receive his week's wages and go home to his mother, a poor widow, whose slender income scarcely sufficed to give food to her little household.

"You needn't come to-morrow, John," said the printer, as he handed the lad the two dollars that were due him for the week's work; "it is Christmas, you know."

The boy took the money, and after lingering a moment, turned away and walked toward the door. He evidently expected something, and seemed disappointed. The

printer noticed this, and at once comprehended its meaning.

"John," said he kindly.

The boy stopped and turned around; as
he did so, the printer took up a half-dollar
from the desk, and holding it between his
fingers, said—

"You've been a very good boy, John,
and I think you deserve a Christmas-gift.
Here's half a dollar for you."

John's countenance was lit up in an instant. As he came back to get the money,
the printer's eyes rested upon his feet,
which were not covered with a very comfortable pair of shoes, and he said—

"Which would you rather have, John,
this half-dollar or a pair of new shoes?"

"I'd rather have the new shoes," replied
John without hesitation.

"Very well; I'll write you an order on
a shoemaker, and you can go and fit yourself;" and the printer turned to his desk
and wrote the order.

As he handed John the piece of paper

on which the order was written, the lad looked earnestly into his face, and then said, with strongly-marked hesitation—

"I think, sir, that my shoes will do very well if mended; they only want mending. Won't you please write shoes for my mother instead of me?"

The boy's voice trembled, and his face was suffused. He felt that he had ventured too much. The printer looked at him for a moment or two, and then said—

"Does your mother want shoes badly?"

"Oh yes, sir. She doesn't earn much by washing and ironing, even when she can do it; but she sprained her wrist three weeks ago, and hasn't been able to do any thing but work a little about the house since."

"And are your wages all that she has to live upon?"

"They are, now."

"You have a little sister, I believe?"

"Yes, sir."

"Does she want shoes, also?"

"She has had nothing but old rags on her feet for a month."

"Indeed!"

The printer turned to his desk, and sat and mused for half a minute, while John stood with his heart beating so loud that he could hear its pulsations.

"Give me that order," the man at length said to the boy, who handed him the slip of paper. He tore it up, and then took his pen and wrote a new order.

"Take this," said he, presenting it to John. "I have told the shoemaker to give you a pair for your mother, yourself, and your little sister; and here is the half-dollar, my boy—you must have that, also."

John took the order and the money, and stood for a few moments looking into the printer's face, while his lips moved as if he were trying to speak; but no sound came therefrom. Then he turned away and left the office without uttering a word.

"John is very late to-night," said the poor Widow Elliot, as she got up and went

to the door to look out in the hope of seeing her boy. Supper had been ready for at
least an hour, but she didn't feel like eating
any thing until John came home. Little
Netty had fallen asleep by the fire, and
was now snugly covered up in bed. As
Mrs. Elliot opened the door, the cold air
pressed in upon her, bearing its heavy bur-
den of snow. She shivered like one in a
sudden ague-fit, and shutting the door
quickly, murmured—

"My poor boy—it is a dreadful night for
him to be out, and so thinly clad. I wonder why he stays so late away!"

The mother had hardly uttered these
words when the door was thrown open, and
John entered with a hasty step, bearing
several packages in his arms, all covered
with snow.

"There's your Christmas-gift, mother,"
said he, in a delighted voice; "and here is
mine, and there is Netty's!" displaying at
the same time three pairs of shoes, a paper

of sugar, another of tea, and another of rice.

Mrs. Elliot looked bewildered.

"Where did all these come from, John?" she asked, in a trembling voice, for she was overcome with surprise and pleasure at this unexpected supply of articles so much needed.

John gave an artless relation of what had passed between him and the printer for whom he worked, and added—

"I knew the number you wore, and I thought I would guess at Netty's size. If they don't fit, the man says he will change them; and I'll go clear back to the store to-night but what she shall have her new shoes for Christmas. Won't she be glad! I wish she were awake."

"And the tea, sugar, and rice, you bought with the half-dollar he gave you?" said the mother.

"Yes," replied John; "I bought the tea and sugar for you. They're your Christ-mas-gift from me. And the rice we'll all have to-morrow. Won't you make us a rice-pudding for our dinner?"

"You're a good boy, John—a very good boy," said the mother, much affected by the generous spirit her son had displayed. "Yes, you shall have a rice pudding. But take off your wet shoes, my son—they are very wet—and dry your feet by the fire."

"No, not until you put Netty's shoes on, to see if they fit her," replied John. "If they don't fit, I'm going back to the store for a pair that will. She shall have her new shoes for Christmas. And, mother, try yours on—may be they won't do."

To satisfy the earnest boy, Mrs. Elliot tried on Netty's shoes, although the child was sleeping.

"Just the thing," said she.

"Now try on yours," urged John.

"They couldn't fit me better," said the mother, as she slipped on one of the shoes. "Now take off your wet ones, and dry your feet before the fire, while I put supper on the table."

John, satisfied now that all was right, did as his mother wished, while she got ready their frugal repast. Both were too much excited to have very keen appetites. As they were about rising from the table, after finishing their meal, some one knocked at the door. John opened it, and a gentleman came in and said familiarly—

"How do you do, Mrs. Elliot?"

"Oh—how do you do, Mr. Mayfield? Take a seat?" and she handed her visitor a chair.

"How has your wrist got, Mrs. Elliot? Are you 'most ready to take my washing again?"

"It's better, I thank you, but not well enough for that; and I can't tell when it will be. A sprain is so long in getting well."

"How do you get on?" asked Mr. Mayfield. "Can you do any kind of work?"

"Nothing more than a little about the house."

"Then you don't earn any thing at all?"

"No, sir—nothing."

"How do you manage to live, Mrs. Elliot?"

"We have to get along the best we can on John's two dollars a week."

"Two dollars a week! You can't live on two dollars a week, Mrs. Elliot; that is impossible."

"It's all we have," said the widow.

Mr. Mayfield asked a good many more questions, and showed a very kind interest in the poor widow's affairs. When he arose to go away, he said—

"I will send you a few things to-night, Mrs. Elliot. This is the season when friends remember each other, and tokens of good-will are passing in all directions. I believe I cannot do better than spend all I designed giving for this purpose, in making you a little more comfortable. So when the man comes with what I shall send, you will know that it is for you. Good night. I will drop in to see you again before long."

And ere Mrs. Elliot could express her thanks, Mr. Mayfield had retired.

No very long time passed before the voice of a man speaking to his horse was heard at the door. The vehicle had moved so noiselessly on the snow-covered street, that its approach had not been observed. The loud stroke of a whip-handle on the door caused the expectant widow and her son to start. John immediately opened it.

"Is this Mrs. Elliot's?" asked a carman, who stood with his leather hat and rough coat all covered with snow.

"Yes, sir," replied John.

"Very well; I've got a Christmas present for her, I rather think; so hold open the door until I bring it in."

John had been trying on his new shoes, and had got them laced up about his ankles just as the carman came. So out he bounded into the snow, leaving the door to take care of itself, and was up into the car in a twinkling. It did not take long, with John's active assistance, to transfer the contents of the car to the widow's store-room, which had been for a long time want-ing in almost every thing.

"Good night to you, madam," said the carman, as he was retiring, "and may to-morrow be the happiest Christmas you have ever spent! It isn't every one who has a friend like yours."

"No—and may God reward him!" said Mrs. Elliot, fervently, as the man closed the door and left her alone with her chil-dren. And now the timely present was more carefully examined. It consisted of many articles. First, and not the least welcome, was half a barrel of flour. Then there was a bag of corn-meal, another of potatoes, with sugar, tea, rice, molasses, butter, etc.; some warm stockings for the children, a cheap thick shawl for herself, and a pair of gum shoes—besides a good many little things that had all been select-ed with strict regard to their use. A large chicken for a Christmas dinner, and some loaves of fresh Dutch-cake for the children had not been forgotten. Added to all this was a letter containing five dollars, in which the generous donor said that on the next day he would send her a small stove and half a ton of coal.

Edward Mayfield slept sweetly and soundly that night. On the next day, which was Christmas, he got the stove for Mrs. Elliot. It was a small, cheap, and economical one, designed expressly for the poor. He sent with it half a ton of coal.

Three or four days after Christmas, Mrs. Green said to Lizzy and Jane, as they sat sewing—

"I declare, girls, we've entirely forgotten our washerwoman, poor Mrs. Elliot. It is some weeks since she sent us word that she had sprained her wrist, and could not do our washing until it got well. I think you had better go and see her this morning. I shouldn't wonder if she stood in need of something. She has two children, and only one of them is old enough to earn any thing

—and even he can only bring home a very small sum. We have done wrong to forget Mrs. Elliot."

"You go and see her, Lizzy," said Jane. "I don't care about visiting poor people in distress; it makes me feel bad."

"To relieve their wants, Jane, ought to make you feel good," said Mrs. Green.

"I know it ought; but I had rather not go."

"Oh yes, Jane," said Lizzy; "you must go with me. I want you to go. Poor Mrs. Elliot! Who knows how much she may have suffered?"

"Yes, Jane, go with Lizzy; I want you to go."

Jane did not like to refuse positively, so she got ready and went, though with a good deal of reluctance. Like a great many others, she had no taste for scenes of distress. If she could relieve want by putting her hand behind her and not seeing the object of penury, she had no objection to doing so; but to look suffering in the face was too revolting to her sensitive feel ings.

When Lizzy and Jane entered the humble home of the widow, they found every thing comfortable, neat, and clean. A small stove was upon the hearth, and, though the day was very cold, it diffused a genial warmth throughout the room. Mrs. Elliot sat knitting; she appeared extremely glad to see the girls. Lizzy inquired how her wrist was, how she was getting along, and if she stood in need of any thing. To the last question she replied—

"I should have wanted almost every thing to make me comfortable, had not Mr. Mayfield, one of the gentlemen I washed for before I hurt my wrist, remembered me at Christmas. He sent me this nice little stove and a load of coal, a half-barrel of flour, meal, potatoes, tea, sugar, and I can't now tell you what all—besides a chicken for our Christmas dinner, and five dollars in money. I'm sure he couldn't have spent less than twenty dollars. Heaven knows

I shall never forget him! He came on Christmas-eve, and inquired so kindly how I was getting along; and then told me that he would send me a little present instead of to those who didn't really need any thing, and who might forgive him for omitting the usual compliments of the season. Soon after he was gone, a man brought us a cart-load of things, and on Christmas-day the stove and coal came."

Jane looked at Lizzy, upon whose face was a warm glow and in whose eyes shone a bright light.

"Then you do not need any thing?" said Lizzy.

"No, I thank you kindly, not now. I am very comfortable. Long before my coal, flour, meal, and potatoes are out, I hope to be able to take in washing again, and then I shall not need any assistance."

"Forgive me, sister, for my light words about Edward," said Jane, the moment she and Lizzy left the widow's house. "He is generous and noble-hearted. I would rather he had done this, than that he should have made me a present of the most costly re-- membrancer he could find, for it stamps his character. Lizzy, you may well be proud of him."

Lizzy did not trust herself to reply, for she could think of no words adequate to the expression of her feelings. When Jane told her father about the widow—Lizzy was modestly silent on the subject—Mr. Green said—

"That was nobly done! There is the ring of the genuine coin! I am proud of him!"

Tears came into Lizzy's eyes as she heard her father speak so warmly and approving- ly of her lover.

"Next year," added Mr. Green, "we must take a lesson of Edward, and improve our system of holiday-presents. How many hundreds and thousands of dollars are wast- ed in useless souvenirs and petty trifles, that might do a lasting good if the stream of kind feelings were turned into a better channel."

"HAVE A DRINK OF COOL WATER, PAPA?"

(7)

THE CUP OF COLD WATER.

HENRY GREEN was a reformed man. He had been a most abandoned drunkard; and, in the years of his sad falling away from sobriety, had shamefully wronged and abused his family. But, in a lucid moment, he perceived with painful distinctness, the precipice upon the very brink of which he was standing, and started back therefrom.

For his suffering wife and children, the waste places became green again, and the desert blossomed as the rose. After a long, long night of weeping, the sun came forth, and his smile brought light and gladness to their spirits. The husband and father was a man once more with the heart of a man. He turned no longer away from them in debasing self-indulgence, but toward them in thoughtful affection.

How quickly is perceived a change for the better in every thing appertaining to the inebriate's family, when the head of it abandons his sin and folly, and returns to his affection and duty. All this change was apparent in the family of Henry Green. They had suffered even to the deprivation of every comfort; but of these one and another were now restored, until every part of their humble dwelling seemed to smile again. How happy they were!

And yet the wife of the reformed man often felt a sense of insecurity. She understood too well that, for her husband, temptation lurked at every point. How often did she await his return home, as evening approached, with trembling anxiety; and mark, while yet afar off, his steps, to see if they were firmly taken!

It was early in the fall of the year when

Henry Green took the pledge. Through the winter, he had worked industriously; and, as he could earn good wages, his income had given them, as just mentioned, very many comforts. He had not been much tempted of his old appetite during the cold weather, nor did he feel its active return at the opening spring. But with the fervent heat of summer, the slumbering desire awoke.

Active bodily labour produced free perspiration. Frequent thirst was the consequence; and, whenever this was felt, the thoughts of the reformed man dwelt upon the pleasure a cool glass of some mixed liquor would give. With an effort, and often with fear at his heart, would he thrust aside the alluring images drawn by his truant imagination. And yet, they would ever and anon return; and there were times when he was tempted almost beyond his strength.

Green was a carpenter. Early in the spring, a gentleman offered him a good contract for putting up two or three frame buildings, which he gladly accepted; and, as the lot upon which his house stood was large, he erected a shop thereon.

More cheerfully and hopefully than ever did the reformed man now work. He saw a clearer light ahead. He would, ere long, recover all he had lost, and even get beyond the point of prosperity from which he had fallen.

Time wore on. Spring passed and the summer opened. July came in with intensely hot weather. Already had Henry Green felt the cravings of his awakening appetite, and it required strong efforts at self-denial to refrain from indulgence.

About eleven o'clock one day—it was a hotter day than usual—Green's thoughts were dwelling, as was now too often the case, upon the "refreshing glass," once so keenly enjoyed. A little way from his shop, though not in view, was a tavern, the bar-room of which memory was picturing to the eyes of his mind with tempting distinctness

He had often been there in times past—often drank there until thought and feeling were lost. He saw, in imagination, the rows of alluring decanters, with their many coloured liquors; he heard the cold ice as it rattled in the glasses; he almost felt the cooling beverage upon his lips. So absorbed did he at length become, that he paused in his work, and leaned over his bench, his eyes half-closed, like one in a dreamy reverie.

It was a moment upon which his future, for good or for evil, hung, trembling in an even balance that a hair might turn.

For as long a time as five minutes did Henry Green stand leaning over his work-bench, a picture of the neighbouring bar-room distinctly before his mind, while he was conscious of an intense thirst, that it seemed as if nothing but a glass of mixed and iced liquor could possible assuage.

With a deeply-drawn breath he at length raised himself, the struggle that was going on in his mind more than half-decided in favour of self-indulgence.

"Papa!" spoke a low, familiar voice by his side.

Green started and turned suddenly. A child, not over four years old, stood by him—a fair child, with a countenance full of innocence and affection. She held a tin cup in both her little hands.

"Have a drink of cool water, papa!"

"Yes, dear," replied the father, in a low voice that was unsteady from the rush of a sudden emotion, and he caught the cup from the child's hands, and, raising it to his lips, drank it eagerly.

Instantly the picture of the bar-room, with all its allurements, faded from the mind of Green. He was a man again, in the integrity of a firm purpose. His child, led to him by the hand of a good Providence, had saved him. The cup of cold water had fully assuaged the violence of his burning thirst; and he was no longer under temptation.

"Thank you, dear!" he murmured, as

he lifted his child in his arms and kissed her tenderly.

"Shall I bring you another cool drink after a while?" asked the little one, as she pressed her father's cheeks with both her hands.

"Did any one tell you to bring me the cup of water?" asked Mr. Green.

"No, sir. But I thought you would like a cool drink," innocently replied the child.

"Yes, dear, bring me another drink after a while." Then kissing the little angel who had been the means of saving him when about to fall into temptation, he replaced her upon the ground, and once more turned to his work; and as he bent his body in labour, he mused thus—

"I did not think of the water when I felt that intense desire for a glass of liquor—it did not seem to be what I wanted. But, the cooling draught sent me (by Heaven, I will say) so opportunely, has quenched the morbid appetite, and I feel it no longer. Water, pure, health-giving water, you are just what I need to give strength to my good resolutions! When the old desire comes again, I will drown it in clear, cold water. I feel safer now. There is a medicine for the inebriate's craving appetite, and it is—WATER. Freely will I use it! THANK GOD FOR WATER!"

THE WOUNDED ROBIN.

THE following is related as the experience of a gentleman who was extremely fond of gunning. For our own part, we haven't shot a bird since our sixteenth year, and never mean to engage in such cruel sport.

Gunning and fishing were my delight when a boy; and, as I grew up toward manhood I followed these inhuman sports with increased pleasure. I could not look upon a bird as it glided through the air, or sat amid the leafy boughs, pouring forth its song, without a murderous desire to destroy its innocent life; and a sight of the water filled me with the spirit of old Izac Walton. Days have I spent alone in the woods with my gun; or in my boat upon the river. But·I have been cured of this sporting passion. Let me relate the manner of the cure.

I have a wife and two children. To preserve the latter from all evil has been the object of my greatest care. Well satisfied as to the effect of external things upon the mind, I have endeavoured, as far as it ·was possible, to preserve them from all contact with forms of vice and crime, and from all debasing influences! With what delight did I watch their infant minds unfolding, like the leaves of a beautiful flower, without the appearance of spot or blemish.

"If we could always keep them as pure," I would sometimes say to their mother—"always as innocent as now! It makes me sad to think how, growing with their growth and strengthening with their strength, certain hereditary inclinations to evil will be gradually developed, and mar the fair face of their spirits. All we can do, is to restrain what is evil and lead them to good. But how difficult the task!"

One day I took a carriage and drove out from the city a few miles, with my wife and two children, to a public-house pleasantly situated near the banks of the Schuylkill. Near the house was a fine grove of trees covering three or four acres of ground, and as I drew up my horse, the clear, strong whistle of a robin reached my ears. Then a woodcock flew across the road. All the sportsman in me was aroused. After accompanying my wife and children into the public parlour and ordering some refreshments, I asked the landlord if he could furnish me with a gun. He had a very fine fowling-piece, which was at my service. With this, in the course of half an hour, I started out, leaving my little ones and their mother to enjoy themselves in the garden; I did not tell them where I was going; nor did they see me with my gun.

For about an hour I enjoyed the sport with all my old enthusiasm. Two brace of woodcock, half a dozen robins, and two or three smaller birds were killed for my pleasure. Recollecting that I had been away from my family longer than was proper, I turned my feet toward the hotel, and was near the edge of the woods, when I saw a robin temptingly perched on a slender bough, and within good shooting-distance. Instantly my gun was at my shoulder. Another second of time, and the innocent bird fell fluttering to the ground. A slight scream and the sound of children's voices, which I knew as my own, followed this act. Then I saw my daughter Anna running to where the bird had fallen, and stoop to lift it from the ground. Her mother sat near, and little Andrew stood by her side.

A sudden regret and shame came over me, and a wish to avoid being known to my children as the one who had shot that bird. A thick clump of bushes hid me from view, and I remained concealed, yet able to see them and near enough to hear their voices.

"Oh, poor, poor bird!" I could hear Anna say, in a tone of pity. "See mother! Its wing is broken! And the blood is on its pretty feathers. What wicked man has hurt the dear, innocent bird?"

And then I saw her raise it tenderly, and lay it softly against her cheek.

The bird, in pain, struggled, and escaping from Anna's hand, fluttered along the ground in the direction of the place where I was crouching to hide myself. I never felt more pain than at this moment. Not for any thing would I have had my child discover in me, her father, the author of the cruel deed over which she was grieving. A few feet from me the wounded bird hid himself in a little bunch of leaves, from which Anna extricated him, and carried him back to her mother.

"Isn't it wicked to shoot the birds which our Heavenly Father has made?" I distinctly heard her ask.

"It is cruel to do so for mere sport," her mother answered.

"It is wicked to be cruel!" said Anna, in a half-inquiring, half-affirmative voice.

"Yes, dear."

"Then the man who shot this bird for sport was a wicked man." Anna's voice was earnest and indignant.

"Let us go back," said my wife, taking our youngest child by the hand. "Perhaps your father has returned and will be waiting for us."

As they moved away, Anna carrying the wounded bird with her, I felt a sense of relief. But my cheeks were burning with shame, for my own child had rebuked me severely. As soon as they were out of sight, I concealed the gun in a spot where a servant could easily find it, threw my birds away, and, taking a wide circuit, went back to the hotel. Never before had I returned with such feelings from a sporting expedition.

Never before had I approached my little family with such a sense of reluctance. They had entered the house, and did not see me approach. On coming into the parlour, I found the wounded robin still in the hands of Anna, who was holding it tenderly against her bosom.

"Oh, papa!" she exclaimed, the moment she saw me, and tears of pity were in her eyes as she spoke, "some cruel man has shot this poor bird. See! its wing is broken."

And she held up to my view the wounded bird, that seemed to shrink closer to her innocent bosom as I drew near. It was the work of my own hands. In seeking for sport, I had wantonly maimed the little songster. I stood silent and rebuked in the presence of my child.

"Wasn't it wicked, father?" said Anna.

"It was a cruel act, dear," I replied, half-turning my face away, to conceal its expression.

"Bang!" shouted my little Andrew, at this moment. He had a stick in his hand, and was pointing at the robin which Anna held to her bosom.

"I've shot him! Now let him fall, Anna," cried the eager child.

"Why, Andrew!" exclaimed his mother,

"*you* wouldn't shoot the dear little bird, would you?"

"Won't you buy me a gun, papa, next Christmas?" said my little boy, not in the least heeding what his mother said. "And then won't I shoot the birds!"

"But it's cruel, Andrew," urged his mother.

"Say, papa, won't you buy me a gun?" he continued, his mind only feeling interest in the imagined sport of shooting, and not having any sense of its cruelty.

After some persuasion, I induced Anna to let me take the wounded bird, and leave it in the care of some one at the hotel, who, in order to satisfy her mind, promised it protection. As we rode home she referred more than a dozen times to the robin, and in every instance denounced the cruelty of the, to her, unknown person, by whom it had been shot. Andrew, on the other hand, thought only of a gun. He carried a stick, and, with it, in imagination, shot more than fifty birds on his way home.

When alone with my wife, on the evening of that day, she said to me—

"How much do I regret the incident of the wounded robin!"

"It afflicted Anna, dreadfully," I remarked.

"Yes, poor child. But I regret it more on Andrew's account."

"I didn't see that it troubled him any."

"And that is just what troubles me."

I was silent, for I now partly comprehended my wife.

"Anna," she went on, "felt that the act of shooting the robin was a cruel one, and the heavenly virtue of pity was awakened in her heart, but Andrew had no sympathy with the suffering bird. All he thought of was a gun, and the thought was the off-spring of a cruel desire to shoot the birds as a matter of sport. Never before had he expressed such a desire."

"But," said I, "merely hearing a gun and seeing a wounded bird, could not have awakened a desire that had no previous existence. It must have been latent there."

"Doubtless, it was, for we are born into all evil desires as latent forms in the mind. But as parents, we are to keep latent these evil inclinations in our children as long as possible, while we seek to quicken into vigorous life all good affections. You know that on the germination of either a good or an evil seed, there instantly takes place an influx of life toward that seed, which is quickly developed into a plant. Good and evil seeds are in the mind, and whichsoever is quickened will grow. Unfortunately, the shooting of that robin in the presence of our little boy, has quickened into life a seed of cruelty, which may grow vigorously, and resist all our efforts to destroy the roots which it will shoot down into the concealed earth of his mind. How tenderly and anxiously do we guard our children, but, alas! how unavailing is sometimes all our care!"

My lips were sealed. I could say nothing in answer, for *I* had done the deed of cruelty—*I* had quickened into life the evil seed. Since that time I have had no desire to partake again of the sportsman's pleasure. Since that time, I have never shot a bird

THE BARGAIN

"WHAT have you there, husband," said Mrs. Courtland to her thrifty and careful spouse, as the latter paused in the open door to give some directions to a couple of porters who had just set something upon the pavement in front of the house.

"Just wait a moment, and I'll tell you. Here, Henry! John! bring it in here," and the two porters entered with a beautiful sofa, nearly new.

"Why, that *is* a beauty, husband! How kind you are!"

"Its second-hand, you perceive; but its hardly soiled—no one would know the difference."

148

"Its just as good as new. What did you give for it?"

"That's the best part of it. Its a splendid bargain. It didn't cost a cent less than a hundred dollars. Now, what do you think I paid for it?"

"Sixty dollars?"

"Only twenty dollars!"

"Well, now, that is a bargain."

"A'n't it, though? It takes me to get things cheap," continued the prudent Mr. Courtland, chuckling with delight.

"Why, how in the world did it go off so low?"

"I managed that. It isn't every one that understands how to do these things."

"But how did you manage it, dear? I should like to know."

"Why, you see, there were a great many other things there, and among the rest some dirty carpets. Before the sale, I pulled over these carpets and threw them upon the sofa; a good deal of dust fell from them, and made the sofa look fifty per cent. worse than it really was. When the sale commenced, there happened to be but few persons there, and I asked the auctioneer to sell the sofa first, as I wanted to go, and would bid for it if it were sold then. Few persons bid freely at the opening of a sale.

"'What's bid for this splendid sofa?' began the auctioneer.

"'I'll give you fifteen dollars for it,' said I; 'its not worth more than that, for its dreadfully abused.'

"'Fifteen dollars! fifteen dollars! only fifteen dollars for this beautiful sofa!' he went on; and a man next to me bid seventeen dollars. I let the auctioneer cry the last bid for a few minutes, until I saw he was likely to knock it down.

"'Twenty dollars!' said I, 'and that's as much as I'll go for it.'

"The other bidder was deceived by this as to the real value of the sofa, for it did look dreadfully disfigured by the dust and dirt, and, consequently, the sofa was knocked off to me."

"That was admirably done, indeed!" said Mrs. Courtland, with a bland smile of satisfaction at having obtained the elegant piece of furniture at so cheap a rate. "And its so near a match, too, for the sofa in our front parlour."

On the day previous to this sale, a widow lady with one daughter, a beautiful and interesting girl about seventeen, were seated on a sofa in a neatly furnished parlour in Hudson street. The mother held in her hand a small piece of paper, on which her eyes were intently fixed; but it could readily be perceived that she saw not the characters that were written upon it.

"What's to be done, ma?" at length asked the daughter.

"Indeed, my child, I cannot tell. The bill is fifty dollars, and has been due, you know, for several days. I haven't got five dollars, and your bill for teaching the Miss Leonards cannot be presented for two weeks, and then it will not amount to this sum."

"Can't we sell something more, ma?" suggested the daughter.

"We have sold all our plate and jewelry, and now I'm sure I don't know what we can dispose of, unless it is something that we really want."

"What do you say to selling the sofa, ma?"

"Well, I don't know, Florence. It don't seem right to part with it. But, perhaps, we can do without it."

"It will readily bring fifty dollars, I suppose."

"Certainly. It is of the best wood and workmanship, and cost one hundred and forty dollars. Your father bought it a short time before he died, and that is less than two years past, you know."

"I should think it would bring nearly a hundred dollars," said Florence, who knew nothing of auction sacrifices; "and that would give us enough, besides paying the quarter's rent, to keep us comfortably until some of my bills come due."

That afternoon the sofa was sent, and on the next afternoon Florence went to the auctioneer's to receive the money for it.

"Have you sold that sofa yet, sir?" asked the timid girl, in a low, hesitating voice.

"What sofa, Miss?" asked the clerk, looking steadily in her face with a bold stare.

"The sofa sent by Mrs. ———, sir."

"When was it to have been sold?"

"Yesterday, sir."

"Oh, we haven't got the bill made out yet. You can call on the day after to-morrow, and we'll settle it for you."

"Can't you settle it to-day, sir? We want the money particularly."

Without replying to the timid girl's request, the clerk commenced turning over the leaves of a large account-book, and in a few minutes had taken off the bill of the sofa."

"Here it is—eighteen dollars and sixty cents. See if it's right, and then sign this receipt."

"A'n't you mistaken, sir? It was a beautiful sofa, and cost one hundred and forty dollars."

"That's all it brought, miss, I assure you. Furniture sells very badly now."

Florence rolled up the bills that were given her, and returned home with a heavy heart.

"It only brought eighteen dollars and sixty cents, ma," said she, throwing the notes into her mother's lap, and bursting into tears.

"Heaven only knows, then, what we shall do," said the widow, clasping her hands together, and looking upward.

Reader! There are always two parties in the case of bargains—the gainer and the loser; and while the one is delighted with the advantage he has obtained, he rarely thinks of the necessities which have forced the other party to accept the highest offer.

THE END.